LOOK BEYOND THE PICTURE

THINGS AREN'T ALWAYS WHAT THEY SEEM

PEGGY MARCEAUX

ISBN: 978-1-956581-21-8   PB

Erin Go Bragh Publishing
Canyon Lake, TX

Manufactured in the United States of America
Book Design by Kathleen's Graphics

Table of Contents

AstroCats
TRAPPED IN SPACE

COWBOY HELL

CHASING
A GHOST

ASTRO CATS

TRAPPED IN SPACE

PEGGY MARCEAUX

AstroCats

The SpaceX Falcon 9 Rocket propelled three spayed cats, called mollies, into outer space. Following John Houbolt's theory, they could use the moon's trajectory and orbit it to save fuel. When they reached the moon's orbit, the Command Module, joined to the Lunar Module, was able to separate away easily. Addison the Maine Coon, Jellyroll, the tabby Manx, and Deuteronomy, the short-haired calico, then launched their retro rockets and began to orbit the moon quietly. When they thought they had found a smooth area to land, for there were lots of bumps, craters and mountains, they landed the Hawk Lunar Module on the surface of the moon.

Since they were all mollies, their attitudes showed it; they were ambitious, decisive and not easily distracted by a tom cat's desires. At least, that's what true mollies were supposed to be.

"The Hawk has landed," Addison relayed to Rodney in the Command Module. Rodney was glad to hear it. He took successes and failures on these missions personally. Professional was his middle name, and he took that personally, too. He was well decorated by the Air Force in that department; medals attached to his uniform proved it.

Each in the Lunar Module unbuckled her belt and floated up out of her seat. Though their packs were cumbersome in the capsule, out of it they felt light. By the sheer size of her, Addison won the rights to step out first. No one would challenge her. After all, these were cats, unaccustomed to the courtesies of human kind. She opened the hatch, then gingerly slipped out of the capsule – with golf ball and club in paw. As she touched down, she said, "that's four small steps for cat kind . . .", then stood on her hind legs and struck the ball with so much force it flew over the moon, just barely missing the cow that was jumping over it at that moment, . . .

"and one giant leap for Tiger Woods." Deuteronomy giggled, thinking, *I'm sure the ball will still be orbiting* the moon tomorrow.

When it was time to plant the flag, Jellyroll and Deuteronomy joined Addison a little ways from the space craft. They dug a hole in the dusty, barren moon with their boots. Deuteronomy read what they had inscribed on it: "We come in peace for all cat kind. Hiss," and she giggled.

Addison rolled her eyes. Dogs would have congratulated them on their phenomenal achievement had they known – or even cared--about it. Jellyroll stood there, still saluting. Suddenly, her salute turned into a finger point.

"Look," she said, "somebody got here before we did. He's fishing in the dust right over there."

Addison and Deuteronomy turned their bodies around to see him. They were flabbergasted to see a man with a very large face fishing. Because there was hardly any gravity pull on the moon, they had to bounce sideways to get to him.

"I feel like a crab," said Deuteronomy.

"Oh, geez, stop it with the ad-libbing," admonished Addison.

When they got to him, they introduced themselves. "Hello, we're from Earth," said Addison.

"Oh, hello. I see you guys staring up at me at night all the time. I'm the man in the moon. I'm fishing for my supper here in Moon River. "

"But there is no river here. You have to have water for a river," Jellyroll looked at him quizzically.

"Then why do you earthlings always sing about it? Youi know, *Moon River*?" That confounded all of the cats.

"I'm moon fishing for a moon fish. Google it. You'll see what it is," replied the man in the moon. "By the way, one man's dust is another cat's water," he answered. "Oh, hang on. I've got a bite." And, he proceeded to show them the 'Art of the Reel.' He struggled with a tight line that shook him every which way. The cats were in awe watching the man in the moon struggle with the tight line, moving from side to side. Finally, one hour later, he managed to land the beast. A beast it was, too. It was almost as big as a whale, only it was a perfect, beautiful circle of a fish. Rainbow colors flashed in it as they curled all around on each other, the colors shimmering on him like sequins. Jellyroll's mouth watered. She loved fish.

"It's the only warm-blooded fish on my planet or yours," added the man in the moon. "It keeps itself warm by flapping its tiny flippers."

"It's almost as big as Addison!" Jellyroll exclaimed.

Addison hopped 180 degrees around to turn on Jellyroll. "What did you say?"

Jellyroll gulped. She didn't think she said it that loud. She thought quickly. "I said it's almost as big as our Madison-Avenue, man–hole-covers."

Soon Beethoven's *Moonlight Sonata* started playing in their helmets, signaling they were almost out of oxygen. So they wished the man in the moon a good supper. Though Jellyroll would have loved to stay and share it with him, instead, he joined the other two and crab-bounced his way back to the Lunar Module. Once inside the Hawk, they removed their head gear and broke out supper: crushed tuna-filled moon pies mixed with water they had to suck out of bags.

"Umm, mmmm," Addison crooned Billie Holiday's tune, *Blue Moon,* and said "Yummy."

Then it was time for a cat nap and a purr or two, where she dreamed about their next mission: the ISS.

The next leg of the journey was the International Space Station, or ISS. Thanks to Houbolt's theory, they had enough fuel to get there. The ISS was made up of four groups of five countries:

(1) NASA (The United States);
(2) JAXA (Japan);
(3) ESA (11 European countries);
(4) CSA (Canada); and
(5) Roscomos (Russia).

The panels on the outside of the station were solar panels for heat because it is very cold in space. The inside is made up of divisions of five canisters, or spheres, for each group, or groups, of countries, though the Astrocats or Cosmokats were not held to just their side of the space craft because they work as a team, they were free to float to whichever section they wanted to visit. Deuteronomy and Jellyroll liked that a lot; Addison, not so much. She was all about control.

Afterward, Addison radioed Rodney on the Command Module that they were ready to orbit and hook up with him again. Rodney radioed back that he had just passed the orbital pick position, so, they would have to wait for another rotation in order to rendezvous. She was a little peeved, but, nonetheless, she answered him with, "Roger that, the Lunar Module is in the waiting mode." Rodney was a stickler for going 'by the book.' He was a small, street-wise, feral cat, but sometimes intimidation came in smaller packages. With him, there was his way and no other way, or so she liked to think. As the cats waited for the rotation of the Command Module, to arrive, they reviewed what they had already learned about the ISS and the EVAs (Extravehicular activities). They were warned that when they crawled out to do maintenance in space, their practice in neutral buoyancy would be tested, meaning that out in space, your body had a natural tendency to fall, though still floating. They were ready and were grateful that paw rails were installed. They were also grateful they had been schooled in the breathing techniques of scuba diving in pressurized suits, *though who ever heard of dunking a cat? Even for space,* thought Addison. *Ridiculous.*

Finally, Rodney broke in with static. "Command Module back to Lunar Module. Addison, ready for the hook-up?"

Addison started the Lunar Module, "Ascending to T-6 orbit."

Once the modules were lined up, Rodney gave the all-clear signal, and the two modules clicked into one another perfectly. Then, it was just a matter of aiming the Command Module toward the ISS, transferring the Lunar Module crew, and Rodney igniting his booster rockets. Because Rodney had to dump the Lunar Module, Addison felt cooped up with Deuteronomy and Rodney for the three-day trip (Jellyroll didn't count). His bushy tail had been as uncomfortable crammed in his spacesuit as Deuteronomy's extra-long one had. When they finally arrived at the ISS, Rodney turned his space vehicle around and docked it in the NASA docking area. The four cats crawled out and were met by a Siamese from Japan, a Russian Blue, and a Dane. Though many countries could be on the ISS, only a few visited it at one time. Finally, they met a hairless,

Canadian Sphynx from Quebec City, whose English language they knew well.

"Hello, my name is Addison."

"Welcome aboard," replied the Sphynx with a French accent.

"My name is Pierre." It was hard not to stare at a cat with no hair.

"I'm Jellyroll," the Manx said, shaking Pierre's bare--paw. Pierre couldn't help but smile at the name.

"Glad to make your acquaintance," replied Pierre. The Siamese and Russian Blue nodded. Deuteronomy stepped up next. "Hi, I'm Deutero—" Suddenly, the ISS was hit with a large meteor that punched a big hole in it. Everyone held on to whatever was around them, but, *shwoop,* Deuteronomy was sucked through the hole's vacuum into space.

"Oh no!" cried Jellyroll. "Deuteronomy is gone!"

After quickly climbing into their oxygen suits, they looked out of the hole and saw Deuteronomy float-dropping. Coming to her senses, Deuteronomy thought, *oh how lucky I was to have refilled my suit with oxygen when I first returned to the Hawk before supper. She was* relieved. *At least now I have three hours to live; I hope in that time they can figure something out to save me.*

Rodney quickly shut his Command-Module hatch and refilled his suit with oxygen, as well. Pierre shoved the Siamese, the Russian Blue, the Dane, Addison and Jellyroll inside the hatch that he could shut off. He shouted for the other Cosmokat and the French Astrocat to hurry.

They were already pulling themselves up the space shafts by the footholds after the loud bang and jolt from the meteor's impact. Rodney had stepped out of his Command Module, and Pierre quickly pulled him in through the protected hatch. By the time the French *Chartreux* and the Russian from Siberia had arrived, Pierre had already devised a plan.

"Deuteronomy is float-dropping helplessly in space about 72.2 meters from the spaceship. I will tether myself to the space craft while all the rest of you will use your tethers as ropes. We think she is completely out of oxygen, which means she won't be able to respond to us. But there is always hope that she aired up on the moon, so let's keep our paw-toes crossed. Okay? I'm out first. Give me time to get a bit acclimated with a good paw hold then come on. I will let Addison, Jellyroll or Rodney go last; that way they will be able to see if she is okay. Just don't get your hopes up. Ready? Here goes."

The plan clicked right as Pierre devised it. He tethered to the space ship without any hic-cups, then it was the Russian Blue, the Siamese, the Russian Siberian, the Danish Norwegian Forest Cat, the French *Chartreux,* Rodney, Addison and Jellyroll; the last eight weren't tethered to anything but the Cosmokat's or Astrocat's tether above him or her. When she made it down to Deuteronomy, Jellyroll didn't know whether she would be conscious, even if she had refilled her oxygen on the moon. Jellyroll floated her tether in front of her and tried communicating through their headgear.

"Deuteronomy? Are you still with us, girl?" *Shhh, cliket, shhh.*

"Static," Jellyroll relayed.

"Deuteronomy, please come in. Are you still with us? Please, come in, Deuteronomy."

"I'm *shhh* can't *clicket.*"

"Oh, did you hear that, Addison?! Rodney?!"

"Yes!" Both voices exclaimed.

"Yes! She must have refueled her suit!" Rodney said, excited.

"Can't reach *shhhh.*"

"Addison, can you stretch some more? She can't reach the tether."

"You're breaking *shhhh* come *shhhh,*" Deuteronomy coughed.

Long silence. Jellyroll wanted to lick the hair on her right shoulder in the worst way. It was a nervous tic.

"Is she still with us?" asked Addison.

"Not sure. Deuteronomy, are you still there?"

"Okay. I've got the *clicket* tether."

"Start hauling her up slowly, gang. I don't want her letting go. We're eating into her time already," Jellyroll stated.

Just then, Jellyroll's space suit was hit by debris. "Oh no!" Snapped Jellyroll. "I've just been hit by something, and I'm losing oxygen!"

Pierre exclaimed: "She's only got seconds; someone get her up here STAT."

Rodney grabbed Jellyroll, put her tether into Addison's paw, and pulled himself up by the tethers. He climbed over every cat in line, pushing himself off to pull-float faster. He finally got above Pierre and into the spaceship, just in the nick of time, for she was gasping for air. But, he had saved her life, and she had developed a new-found appreciation for him. With one emergency abated; they could now work to save Deuteronomy. They slowly, carefully, pulled her up into the damaged spacecraft that they would have to work on the rest of the day, and probably into the night, to repair. Deuteronomy barely had the strength to crawl back through the hole the meteor had made, but her comrades were behind her and pushed her in. Once in, they temporarily placed a metal panel over the hole and celebrated with lots of hugs.

They all turned away and aired up their space suits, again, except for Deuteronomy. They had some maintenance work to do repairing the meteor hole.

Deuteronomy was suffering from a bad case of vertigo, so Jellyroll, Addison and Rodney covered her shift. They had to carefully, float outside of the craft to get the job done, all their tools tethered to them as they were tethered to it. It was a giant job, but that's what they trained for. Olav, the Dane, hung back for a bit

After they repaired the hole, they ate some chicken salad in tubes. They didn't have the strength to do much else but crawl into their sleeping bags in a small flat closet on the Quest floor, designated for each of them. They were anxious to catch a few Zzzzs. They knew they had some hard days ahead of them before they had to put weather stations in space by way of Artemis. They had checked their return space craft, the Russian Soyuz, and noticed how compact it was. They had been trained for that, too.

Finally, they could ditch their suits and could free their tails. That was such a relief to Addison and Deuteronomy. It was funny watching all those cats' vestibular senses trying to right themselves as if on earth. They floated around, but were often overcome by a natural sense to defy zero gravity and drop their legs. They enjoyed the comradery of the foreign Astrocats and Cosmokats, as well. They enjoyed working with them and getting to know them. Sometimes, they thought the foreigners were a bit disingenuous, though, such as the time the Russian Blue purposely spoke in his native tongue when greeting Addison. Raskolnikov, the Blue, waved to Addison, smiling and said to Boris, the Siberian, *"Осторожно, ведьма вернулась --"* (Watch out, the witch is back). At which Boris replied, *"c густым веником"* (with a bushy broom). The two would smile amiably as if they had just wished her a beautiful morning. Addison smiled back, but she didn't know what they'd said; she didn't trust them one bit.

Jellyroll enjoyed being out of her spacesuit, too. She could spin the plastic, soda-can holder on her front leg that her friends from the wharf gave her as a memento. She loved those cats and what they were doing for the Earth: cleaning it up one piece of plastic at a time. Their most enjoyable room on the spacecraft was what the Astrocats called the "dome"; it was a 360-degree, bay window that allowed the Astrocats to see, well 360 degrees of the entirety of space.

"Wow!" said Jellyroll, "look at earth! It's gorgeous up here two hundred and forty-four miles away!"

Jellyroll was now fully recovered from her near-death experience, and smiled continuously. She licked the hair on her right shoulder a couple of times out of habit, and spun the plastic circle on her front leg just above her right paw.

"I know," added Deuteronomy, now completely recovered from her scare, though she was still fighting her vertigo. After they finished "oooing "and "aaahing," they pulled their way back to the US Harmony room, by way of the floor footholds, to start the new day's two-hour workouts. They had to offset microgravity that atrophied muscle and decreased bone mass. In the US Harmony room they had a bicycle, a treadmill with harness with a bungee cord to stay on it, and a resistance machine for weight lifting. They used a timer, and each did sixty-five-minute exercise shifts, which would give them five minutes to switch to another piece of equipment.

"I love the bicycle best," said Jellyroll.

Since they had no orientation in outer space, there was no up and no down, except what they made of it. Therefore, a cat's front legs could be on the pedals of a bike, and her hind legs on the handle bars, and blood wouldn't rush to her head. All she had to do was make sure her tail wouldn't get caught in the spokes. But, that was no problem for a Manx, since she had no tail.

"All the floating was fun. The floor holds could help keep you in place, too, so you don't float away when you don't want to," said Jellyroll. "But they could give you blisters on top of your feet if you aren't careful. You can also pull yourself up a canister shaft with them; that's fun, too!

My 'most funnest' thing to do out of everything, though, is to curl up on my sleeping bag, with my hind paw in a cord to hold me in place, way in the back of my flat closet, and take a bath. I love to lick my paw and clean the backs of my ears, my whiskers and my face, then lick the hair on my back and stay clean. That makes me purr the most."

Addison wasn't concerned about what made her feel clean on the ISS. She was daunted by the size of the Danish, Norwegian Forest Astrocat. He was huge, almost as big as she was. She didn't like being intimidated. All she wanted to do was get through these missions and back to her own turf, where she could surround herself with all the smaller cats in her territory. She was a massive Maine Coon, after all, an American domesticated breed which struck fear in any other breed who crossed her path. They gave her a wide berth, and she liked that. It was good to be the top Molly of the Walk, and she missed it. For now, she settled on squishing a tuna patina paste out of its tube into her mouth and crawling into her sleeping bag. Typical of her species, Addison loved nothing more than a dark, close space, even if she hated to admit to being normal in any way. Tonight, she would fall asleep to a nightingale song in her ears. Tomorrow she would wake after eight hours of sleep to a bevy of medical tests.

Deuteronomy was content this evening to read her favorite book, A Cat's Tale: A Journey Through Feline History. All the Astrocats and Cosmokats showed her nothing but courtesy and pity this evening for what she had endured, and she so appreciated what they had done for her. She curled over carefully on her back, trying to keep the vertigo at bay, remembering to slip her hind leg into a cord that would hold her in place. She held the book on her chest so it wouldn't float away and remembered a sweet exchange she had had earlier with the Dane, Olav, the Norwegian Forest Cat; a tom, though she was a molly, she seemed to have an odd attraction to.

A rush of headiness came over her. She didn't know if it was the exchange with Olav or the vertigo that brought it on. He had strolled over to her after her ordeal, pointed to her tail and smiled. "That's a pretty tail."

"Well, for one thing it's longer than most," she'd started, after wrapping it around herself. She was always self-deprecating where her tail was concerned.

He shook his head and asked inquisitively. "Long?" He repeated her word with a wonderful accent.

"Yes," she said, "you know, from here to here," and she suggested its length.

"Ingen," he had said, shaking his head and smiling. "No," He looked up, pursed his lips in thought, then said, "purr-ty."

"Oh, well, *thank you.*"

"You're velcome." He nodded and then hurriedly walked away, still in his space suit, to join the others outside.

He's so regal. That cat puts Addison to shame, she thought. He's so handsome, too. What beautiful kittens we could have made. Then, sadly, she turned the page in her book.

The next morning, they stayed to a routine and floated to the US Harmony to begin their exercise training.

"I've got dibs on the treadmill," shouted Addison. Deuteronomy and Jellyroll looked at one another; Jellyroll just shrugged, but Deuteronomy laid her ears back. After the gracious treatment she had received from Olav, she was sick of Addison's bossiness. Deuteronomy reached the treadmill first and took hold of the bungee cords and harness that would hold her in place. Addison grabbed Deuteronomy's long tail and pulled her back.

"Oh no, you don't."

"Oh, yes I do," and she started to buckle the harness on herself. That was all it took for the Full Feline Face-Off to commence: they turned their sides to one another, bodies and tails humped up and bristled, ears flattened, teeth exposed, and mouths hissing. It was on! The spitting, the snarling and the screaming started. There ensued the wildest, loudest, cat-scratching fight one could ever imagine. It all started with Addison's "hisssss, grrrowl, and then meeeowal!" They floated away from each other at times, but not for long. Jellyroll licked her right shoulder hair four times.

"*Mon Dieu,*" (my God) cried Gustave, the French *Chartreux*. "*Quels chats grossies*" (what crass cats).

It would have been nice if Pierre could have just thrown a bucket of water on them, but you can't do that in space. Pierre ended it instead by banishing them from the Harmony Room.

"You and Deuteronomy will begin to pay us back in the urine lab tomorrow," he said to Addison.

"You two will make us the bucket of water it would have taken to break you up," replied Pierre.

"Me? Make water from urine?"

Pierre looked hard at Addison. Addison knew then never to toy with him.

In the end, they had scratched, bitten into necks and just generally ruined their resolve to exercise rationally. So, they floated from the Harmony room dejected and embarrassed, the irony of the room's name completely lost on them. They passed Boris, the Siberian and Raskolnikov, the Russian Blue Cosmokats; Hiakara, the Japanese Siamese; Gustave, the French *Chartreux;* Olav, the Danish Norwegian

Forest Cat; and Pierre, the Sphynx Canadian from Quebec City Astrocats, who tried and sentenced them, before they passed Rodney and Jellyroll.

Jellyroll licked her right shoulder hair four times. Deuteronomy and Addison floated straight for the medic station before going to their sleeping bags in the US' Quest room, to lick their wounds and their pride.

"You know," said Pierre, "I don't think we've ever had an episode like that on board before.

C'est est Américains pour toi," he announced, finally using his Quebec City French. (That's Americans for you).

"Tellement vrai," agreed Gustave (so true).

Jellyroll, meanwhile, had enjoyed the uninterrupted, two-hour workout the next morning: her resistance exercise devise for weight lifting, her bungee cord and harness workout on the treadmill and her favorite, the bicycle. She was now good to go. She intended to spend the remainder of her day checking out the labs, especially the Russian labs which were the oldest on the space station. She was most interested in the system of electrolysis. She wanted to know how they conducted electricity from the solar panels and split water into oxygen and hydrogen.

She licked her right shoulder twice and spun the plastic on her leg; however, she was quickly corralled by Pierre.

"Jellyroll, would you mind suiting up and going out to check the outside of the canisters for asteroid damage?"

"No. What? Alone?"

"It's not a scary thing to.do. We do it all the time here. Just go see if there is any buildup of abrasions or pieces of asteroid that need to be scraped off the canisters. It's just ordinary maintenance work," reassured Pierre.

"Okay. I've got this," and Jellyroll went off to put on her spacewalk suit.

Unfortunately for Addison and Deuteronomy, they weren't going to see anything but their sleeping bags, for early the next morning they were floating to the urine, sweat and condensation lab to purify it all into the amount of water that Pierre deemed appropriate to atone for their fight. They wouldn't admit it, but they were both mighty sore.

While outside the space craft, sometime later, Jellyroll was struggling for air. She radioed her condition to Pierre.

"Come back in here quickly," ordered Pierre. "We need to check this out ASAP."

There was no quickly to it. Jellyroll had to pull-float her way back around and into the entrance-exit chamber, gasping at times. Once inside, Jellyroll's suit was carefully examined. Pierre found striations on her gloves that suggested, while she was making her way down the handrails, those handrails had been damaged by pieces of broken asteroids as well.

"Looks like you're going to have to go out and scrape the handrails, too," said Pierre. "Now be really careful where you put your hands on the rails, and put on a fresh suit first."

Meanwhile, on the way to the urine lab, Addison and Deuteronomy encountered some of the ISS crew.

"I'm sorry for my part in this stink last night," Deuteronomy told them, her head down.

"You sure are," affirmed Addison, unwilling to claim her part in it. Still, the crew knew who they'd be willing, to house again, and with whom they would fly, in the future. It took them all day long to make just one-half a bucket of water, which meant they knew who'd they be working with and at what tomorrow.

When Jellyroll had finished scraping the asteroid pieces from the outside of the canisters, and off the handrails, she re-entered the hatch of the spaceship. Pierre met her as she came in.

"Thank you, Jellyroll, for contributing your part to the ISS as a NASA crew member. Addison and Deuteronomy were embarrassments, and your work will counterbalance that," offered Pierre.

Jellyroll smiled at him, changed out of her spacesuit, licked the hair on her right shoulder twice in satisfaction, spun the soda plastic around her right leg and pull-floated herself over to the Russian Laboratory as was planned before Pierre intervened.

The day they had finished their 'prison sentence,' Deuteronomy and Addison were instructed to go to the lab where the ESA did medical testing. Olav led Addison in to get an EKG. He shaved her chest, put electrode patches on it, and connected the heart-monitor cables to them. He then pinned Addison to the wall with bungee cords and hooked her up to the heart monitor on the computer. Then, the EKG was started. Suddenly, Olav stared at the monitor, his eyes, squinting then looking all around the computer screen. Suddenly, they grew wide. Olav stared at the screen in disbelief. Addison started to feel very uncomfortable.

"No wonder!" said Olav, "This cat has no heart. She's the Tin Man in the Wizard of Oz," he said, chuckling at his own joke.

Addison became so angry she shook.

The two Russians stepped in about this time and saw Addison pinned to the wall. They also saw Deuteronomy and then Jellyroll playing with the soda-can plastic around her leg.

Boris said to his fellow Cosmokat, "The big kat was to blame for their fight." He pointed to Deuteronomy and said, "She is so much smaller than that big one is."

Raskolnikov replied with, *"Глупая Молли"* (Stupid molly). They then laughed at what Raskolikov had said.

Addison had had enough. She started pulling the bungee cords off of her.

Deuteronomy and Addison looked at one another. Jellyroll licked her right shoulder twice. They'd made a fool out of Addison, and she didn't like it one bit, but it wasn't until they rubbed up against Deuteronomy to show their support for her, and then licked her face, that Addison lost it. Her neck veins bulged, and she ripped the heart-monitor cables off her chest. She stomped back in the direction of the NASA quarters, Jellyroll following close behind and licking the hair on her right shoulder.

"Bunch of dumb toms!" Addison spat, looking over her shoulder.

Deuteronomy still wasn't comfortable being around Addison, so she hung back and stared at the heart monitor, seeing that, indeed, there was heart activity on it. She smiled at the joke Olav made about the Tin Man and the Wizard of Oz. She had no idea what Raskolnikov said, though, she could imagine it was an insult.

That night was a big one for the US space crew, for they would be flying back to Earth early the next morning. Since NASA had suspended its space program, it always used the Russian Soyuz to fly in and out of space. When morning came, Deuteronomy exchanged addresses with Olav, for she would miss him, and she wanted to study his language. Once it was time to board the craft, Jellyroll was pushed into it right after Deuteronomy, just so Addison could save some semblance of pride. It was quite a squeeze with the three of them and Rodney to boot.

"Move over, Jellyroll!" Addison hissed.

"Move where?" was Jellyroll's reply; she wanted to lick her shoulder, but she couldn't through a spacesuit.

"Over!" and Addison pushed her into Deuteronomy.

"For gosh sakes, let me have room for my insides, will ya?" Deuteronomy demanded.

"Looks like your pal here is playing favorites." Addison turned to look at Jellyroll.

"Keep me outta this," said Jellyroll looking at both of them.

Addison snorted. "Looks to me you're right in the middle of it."

Not even out of the gates, and Addison had returned right back to her old self, thought Deuteronomy.

Rodney knew better than to open his mouth; *mollies,* he thought.

Just as the retro-rockets burned away some two hours later, the parachutes on the Soyuz deployed, and the cats fell to the appointed spot in the Pacific. The "Dragon's Nest" was there within minutes to pick them up; from there they were moved to a helicopter and flown to recliners. The aeronautical space Air Force Academy didn't want to risk breaking any bones, although the cats weren't at the space station that long. Still, they risked the pull of gravity pretty soon by telling the Astrocats they only had a short time to get in shape before their most challenging mission yet; they kept it a secret from others because they were going to have to travel faster than the speed of light to get there. Jellyroll, however, was excited about it. It was a 1,470 light-year-travel-time trip to check out what was going on with the Tabby Star – right in Jellyroll's wheelhouse, since she herself was a tabby Manx. The star was named after the LSU Professor who discovered it, Tabetha Boyajian. It was also numbered Star KIC 8462852, in Sept., 2015.

Due to weather reasons a little over a month's time passed before the Artemis was launched. Our same foursome was picked to go to on these next three missions. There was some haggling about it because ISS sent word that Addison's behavior was questionable, and it had reached all the way up the Air Force chain of command. However, they accepted her apologies and believed her when she said that, "nothing like that would ever happen again." And, believe it or not, it didn't, at least not as far as the Air Force was concerned. So, the same Astrocats boarded the Artemis Lunar Module, and the Command Module, above the powerful Rocket for its maiden voyage, with passengers.

After a long ride, they could see the dimness and brightness of the Tabby Star coming and going, blinking at about 22%. The Lunar and Command Modules radioed each other back and forth.

"What's causing that?" asked Jellyroll through her head gear.'"

"That's what we are here to find out," answered Addison.

Rodney let the rocket burn away and piloted the Command Module, "This time we are going to disengage MEDLI (Mars Entry, Descent and Landing Instrument), and let it drop down to check out the star temperature and the surface pressure."

"Roger that," replied Addison.

"Look," exclaimed Jellyroll. "It seems like someone has built layers of clear glass over the star. What might that be?"

They all stared hard, trying to fathom an answer.

"Could be dust particles, or pieces of asteroids rimming the star," proposed Rodney.

"Or, maybe aliens put a megastructure with panels on the star to steal the heat of the sun for their own warmth," dubiously hypothesized Deuteronomy, staring hard at the structure.

"That seems pretty far-fetched, but let's get Perseverance over there, since MEDLI reported back that the temp is tolerable for it. and check it out," ventured Rodney, and he prepared to launch the Rover.

After receiving data back from the Rover, they had something to report.

Well," said Rodney, "it's pretty clear from Perseverance's perspective that the cache rocks were moved into some sort of alignment, which supports Deuteronomy's theory."

"Oh, man," cried out Addison. "Look at these readings!"

"What aliens could these be?" asked Jellyroll.

"From some planet in the Cygnus Constellation, I imagine," replied Rodney. "Well, let's pick up the MEDLI and skedaddle," ordered Rodney. "Don't want anyone seeing us here."

"What about Perseverance? Won't they know America made it?" asked Jellyroll.

"Not unless they watch Earth's television and read our newspapers," answered Rodney. "We need to report this back to NASA." With that mission completed, the Artemis crew was looking forward to the next one: returning to the moon, and then going to Mars, to put some weather stations in place.

It was like old times orbiting the moon. The lunar cats all looked forward to seeing their friend, the man in the moon, again. Their mission was about weather this time, but little else that they knew of. When they landed, they didn't see him until they were setting up the weather-station in the crater the Asteroid GH2 made in April of 2020. It was solid iron in there, and the tower would stand up several meters high.

"What are you doing?" asked the man in the moon, surprising them.

"Oh, hey. We didn't know where you were." Jellyroll told him. "I didn't see you fishing."

"I was in my usual place, smiling at the earth," the man in the moon replied.

"Well, we are excited to tell you that earth has sent us back here, and then to Mars, to set up weather stations," Addison answered him.

"What for?"

Addison was annoyed that he had to answer such a stupid question with such an obvious answer.

"What for? Why to monitor the earth's weather, that's what for."

"So, again, I ask you, what for?" Deuteronomy looked at the man in the moon curiously.

Addison stood up straight and looked him right in the eyes, trying to decide if this was a trick question, and he had missed something.

"Remember," he said, "I'm in charge of the tides on your planet. I know something about that melting ice in both the north and south poles, about all that plastic in the oceans you've been feeding your fish, about all that plastic in your landfills that won't have time to erode, about all those carbon emissions with which you've been poisoning your air, about all those wildfires you can't stop, about all those floods you can't shore up, about all those earthquakes swallowing up millions in third-world countries, not to mention the imminent threat of a nuclear-plant meltdown or bomb, and all the climate change your people have been turning a blind eye to."

The Astrocats had furled their brows by now.

"So, I ask you again," the man in the moon said to them, "why this weather station? Why now, when it could be too late?"

Finally, Deuteronomy answered the question. "Our superiors sent us here, to help turn the tide."

None of the cats spoke after that; each was alone in her own thoughts.

"Humph," replied the man in the moon. "There's nothing you can do to turn something as big as this 'tide'. You may as well turn around and go back. You can't live here, and you can't live on Mars."

"No?" asked Addison. "And they are crashing the International Space Station in the Pacific in 2031."

"More food for the fish," continued the man in the moon.

The Astrocats all looked at one another, as if to ask, *is this true? If so, what do we do? We* can't stay here; we can't live on Mars; we can't live on the ISS since it'll be crashing in '31. What do we do if there is no earth to go home to?

"But, it's not over," rebutted Deuteronomy. "We can still act. We can get involved," she said. "Now that we know how dire it is."

"How?" asked the man in the moon. "You're just cats."

"There are many more of us than there are humans. Don't sell us short. We can network," argued Deuteronomy.

"Yeah," said Addison. "I'm in charge of a whole block of felines, and they travel far and wide."

"And my folks work on boats and at the seashore," added Jellyroll. "They can pick up lots of plastic. Plus, we can offset some of the plastic by chumming good organic food."

With heavy hearts they told the man in the moon goodbye, and side-hopped back to their Lunar Module. They contacted Rodney in the Command Module and told him what they had just learned. "Hogwash," he had said, then they contacted their base; the weather that delayed the launch had already inundated Florida up to Fort Meyers. When they tried to contact NASA, things weren't much better there. They were told by the Air Force to go ahead to Mars and then come home.

Addison told her two other crew members. "Cats and water don't mix. Neither do cats and fire. I don't know what I'm going to do. Except, I will lead my turf cats into stopping deforestation by encouraging recycling. And, we'll look out for sparks caused by vehicles, smokers, chains, etc."

Jellyroll, tried to lick the hair of her right shoulder right through her suit. "I'm going to join my shore-line, plastic collectors and chumming, that's for sure," and she spun the plastic on her leg.

"Then, let's DO something about all this," said Deuteronomy, definitively. "I'm gonna become a Climate Pioneer; that is, join a group that removes

CO_2 (Carbon Dioxide) from the air. They do it by way of a direct air capture box, and pump the CO underground. That, and I'm going to help plant trees."

"Me and my turf cats will join you there," said Addison.

Deuteronomy sat in her chair and buckled up, preparing for their rendezvous with the Command Module. She stared straight out the window at Pollux, the brightest star in the Gemini Constellation closest to the moon. *"Could be,"* she thought, *is not definite. There's still a chance for us to change things. All we have to do is want to.* She sat there and wished upon that star with all her heart, promising to do her part to save the Earth when she returned. But, the man in the moon's question: "How? You are just cats," continued to haunt her all the way home. *Here's hoping at least one of my nine lives will make this a better place. All I need is one. That, in and of itself, gives cats better odds than humans.*

COWBOY HELL

Tex and Sam met training for this flight to Enceladus, one of Saturn's moons. The mission called for SpaceX to launch them the Monday after their training ended, and, following the exploration by Cassini, a robotic sent into space by NASA, and the Italian Space Agency, to research Saturn's moons and rings for life resources. Saturn is the sixth planet from the sun and the second largest after Jupiter, both gaseous planets, though there was evidence that some of Saturn's moons were solid, Cassini was to assure them that Enceladus would, indeed, be solid and could sustain life. Also, because there was little for the men to do on the planet to benefit science, besides keeping records of temperature, barometric pressure, and it's response on the human body, SpaceX needed to provide them with something else to do, so they had them mixing colors for the Borealis. Both men thought it a menial job to work with the Borealis, but they could use it as a jumping board to better, much more prestigious jobs, since it involved experience on Enceladus.

They had also brought with them YesterStone and 1884 CDs to stream and a wrought-iron, calf dummy with a lariat for entertainment. It was a good thing they did, for later they would be met with a lassoing challenge. After donning their spacesuits, they strapped into Falcon 9 and, then, were successfully launched; this was Tex's second time at being offered a job in space, so he took it. It would be Sam's first, and he wasn't complaining –yet. They settled in on the moon, Enceladus, and were pleased with their sleeping arrangements. Tex crashed, he was so exhausted after planning and packing for the flight.

"Hey, Tex, what's that thing out there comin' at us faster than I can draw my six-shooter?"

Tex squinted his eyes, but not for long. Soon his eyes were the size of saucers.

"I think that's a meteor, Sam. We need to get outta here fast." Tex whistled to Rocky; he didn't wait to tighten the cinch. He just pulled himself up on the horse and kicked him hard

"Let's get the hell outta here, boy!

"Where ya goin' Tex?" Sam raised his eyebrows.

"Anywhere but here."

Rocky took off from the moon and rode the vacuum in space all the way to Mars before Tex let him stop. He was panting so badly his mouth was lathering.

"Wish I could find you some water, boy. This here space is no place for a cowboy and his horse."

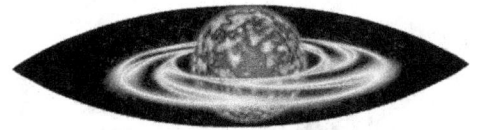

"Hey, wake up, Tex. You were mumblin' somethin' in your sleep," Sam said while putting on his spacesuit.

"Ah, why did ya wake me up, Sam? I was straddlin' my horse, who I am missin' more than my favorite beer." Tex complained.

"Now that's a ride I'd like to have. Your favorite beer that is." Sam said grudgingly.

"What are we doin' today for you to need your spacesuit?" Tex asked him. Text tried to rub the sleep outta his eyes. Dreaming 'bout Rocky was so real to him, and he already missed that horse so much.

"I'm going out to check the back of the place. Just hope I don't freeze my butt off. This place is so dang cold," Sam answered him.

"Oh, no, you don't, Sam. Not without me," Tex looked at him sideways. "I thought you said we had work to do?" Tex continued. "Like colors?"

"Yeah, alright," Sam. told him, "but I want to see what the other side of this bulding looks like first."

While Sam went to look around the corner he slipped on the ice, "Dang," he said, and caught hold of he building on his way down. Tex saw him fall and gingerly walked towards him.

"Are you okay, Sam?" he asked.

"Yeah, just hurt my feelings," Sam answered him.

"Looks like we'll have to entertain ourselves a hell af a lot *in* that cabin," Tex figured out loud.

"I think you're right, Tex. Which is why they gave us that dang Borealis job to do. I hate the idea; may as well have given us a dang puzzle. I'd much prefer girls, he smiled.

"I'd feel a lot better if we can name it the **OK** Borealis. Ya, know, give it a little western flare."

After talking to one another, earlier, they discovered they were both big country western fans.

"Oh, heck, yeah," proclaimed, Sam. "I like that. Dang, I like that a lot."

After the two men carefully made their way back inside, they went to work on the Borealis. Someone had to be in charge of mixing the color shades to make them blend and look different colors of red, blue, purple, green, turquoise, violet, white and pink. It wasn't easy making it happen just right.

Tex was put in charge of that because he had experience with paint, so he had become master of the kaleidoscope, so to speak. Sam's work was more that of hitching colors to the hitching postcards for people to buy; I guess you would call that taking pictures and marketing them. Sometimes he'd have to ask himself "What would John do?" looking for a a "Wayne--Wayne" solution. *John Wayne*, he thought *would get a girl, and not fiddle with these dang color cards,* he'd told himself.

Tex tried mixing orange, blue and green again and kept coming up with these hideios brown, even when introducing a mint green and a violet to it. They were trying to find a pretty brown, but to no avail. Sam went back to the color chart and played with it a bit more. It was helpful that Tex had done some western painting and sold them for big bucks at a store in New Mexico. Mixing paint on the pallet gave you much more freedom than coming up with these shades here on the OK Borealis. That's the night Sam added a load of gun powder to the paint to "put a little more pep in Tex's step." The explosion scared Tex half to death, but he swore to Sam he'd never tell SpaceX about Sam's recklessness. He sure lorded it over him, though.

"The one good thing 'bout the Borealis is that you didn't get smudged up with paint on yer clothes." said Tex.

While Sam played with the color chart, he asked Tex, "Do ya eva wish we had more people here at the Borealis?"

Tex was lost in thought, thinking about the colors, and answered inattentively. "Huh? I guess so." Then he looked up suddenly. "Why" Tex asked.

"Cuz ah do." Sam replied. "Not that ah don't love the company, cuz ah do. But, cuz we might could get a poker game goin' or somthin' other than workn' with these dang colors all the time. Plus, we could raise a lil hell once in a while. I tell ya, I was hoping we could find something daring to do in space, rather than working with these dang colors."

"Yeah," agreed Tex. "Ah see your point, but, no more gun powder."

"And, a girl or two, would be nice," Sam confessed, ignoring the gun powder comment.

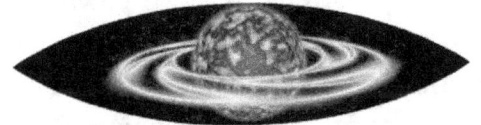

But there weren't more than two of them working at the Borealis, the OK Borealis—ever. Way too many people for Tex, and not nearly enough for Sam. Real early one morning, Sam and Tex heard a thunderous roar of hooves. They both were startled from their beds and looked outside.

"Tell me, Sam, am I havin' another one of those dreams?" Tex ask him.

"No, ya are not, but, ah sure wish ya were."

In the distance, they saw a herd of black cattle with yellow eyes coming at them--a stampede.

"No one even seems to be drivin' 'em. Wonder how they can run round like that without oxygen, and someone tryin' to keep 'em together?" asked Sam.

"Beats me, but I sure would have brought Rocky along if I had known this," Tex replied, ruefully. "What's happenin' out there?" asked Tex.

"Wish ah knew what to tell ya," Sam stood staring at the cattle racing through the sky.

The cattle looked like death itself, with yellow eyes, smoking brands and fire rushing from their nostrils. They cowered the two cowboys. Suddenly, the drover came within sight. It was none other than the ghost of Wyatt Earp. You could see right through him, except for the pistols hanging off his hips and the lariat in his hand. He hung over his quarter horse, to shout, because that stampede was mighty noisy. They would never forget how his voice quivered.

"I drove this herd by here on my way to hell, to tell you, if you don't change your ways, your headed the same direction: straight to Cowboy Hell."

"But you aren't headin' down, like we've been told hell is. Your goin' east," Sam remarked. "And how would you know if we are cowboys," Sam asked.

"There is another hell, made just for cowboys and the like, and I can see in your hearts you are cowboys." Earp answered and laughed hideously, his voice quivering like a weird harmonica sound.

After hearing his remarks, they became so nauseous they just earped right on their boots. Once relieved, they drew their guns on the cattle and tried cutting them down from the beginning of the herd. Tex opened fire on the ghost cattle until his six shooter was empty; he knew he would have surely gotten one. So, he stopped.

Sam kept shooting. In fact, he reloaded and kept firing.

"Something is wrong here, Sam," Tex said. "They aren't falling."

"Tex told him, "I think we're shooting at ghosts—just wastin' our bullets.

"Is that what is happening? Ah figured ah was a better shot than this anyway."

Tex and Sam looked at one another.

"Then you gonna do this, Sam? Be a good man?"

"Are you?" Sam returned the question.

"What would John do?" Tex asked.

"Not this. Ah don't wanna go to any hell; Ah want to live, like His Cock and that Arp guy. We need to live before we die, and, hell, this Borealis thing is just a job. Ah don't wanna be responsible for makin' the world feel better bout things cuz they 'ooo' and 'ahhh' at the Borealis colors. Ah don' care how they feel; Ah care 'bout how *ah* feel." Sam took a deep breath after that long rant.

Trying not to think about what just happened, they spent their spare time fast drawing against each other, at which Tex would usually win because his "Ruger New Vaquero was a smaller pistol than the Sam's Colt, therefore, faster," or so Sam said. That, streaming the CD's and roping the calf all occupied some of their free time. Until, one day, while Tex was lying on his bed and perusing the *Scientific News Magazine*, he paused and shouted, "Whoa!!"

Naturally, that got Sam's attention. "Look at this!" said Tex, and he held the article out for Sam to see without taking his eyes off of it. There was a picture of a flaming planet facing the printed page. Tex didn't wait for him to start reading. "It says NASA has discovered a planet, through its Spitzer Telescope, out to the east side of the solar system, that is twice the size and 18 times the mass of earth. It's called 55 Cancri e, and it orbits a star it is so close to it can do it in just 18 hours. That star is 40 light years away from earth in the Cancer Constellation; 55 Cancri e is half solid and half liquid fire." He looked up at Sam. The article says the "The lava fire measures 2500 degree Celsius on average, and the solid part, 1100." Tex's eyes grew large. "Thing is," he said, "the heat on the planet is gettin hotter and hotter, and they aren't sure why. They don't know where the extra heat is coming from."

"Ah know from where," replied Sam. "From all that beef that's burnin' up since Arp drove the cattle there. That's gotta be Cowboy Hell."

"Ah think your right," agreed Tex.

"I feel the 'dare'in space I wanted to experience is playing right into our hands," concluded Sam.

That article excited them so much that they broke out the six-pack of Tex's 24-oz. cans of *Glazed Cowboy Lager* and drained every last bit of it.

"Wish we had some 'Enceladus', chips and salsa to eat with it." Tex said, and they both laughed out loud.

Feeling pretty good by now, they tried roping the wrought-iron dummy, again. still, with no luck, but they sure laughed a lot. Then, while reaching for his third beer on the outside step, Sam noticed a comet coming their way. He turned to Tex and bet him he couldn't lasso it. Well, the dare was all it took. Tex hurriedly put on his spacesuit, which gave them something else to laugh at, "oh, gimme my hat," he said before he went outside with his lasso. He swung it round and round over his head as the comet neared him. Sam thought to put on his space suit in case he lost the bet, and, wouldn't you know it, he did. He managed to grab the end of the lasso just as Tex caught the comet. It was a good thing, too, because Tex was pulled off the Enceladus, taking Sam with him. They were pulled through the vacuum of space with such enormous speed, it was all they could do to hang on. They flew past meteors and planets and stars. Suddenly, they saw this huge circle of planetary matter with a great, dark center. The comet seemed to be heading right for it. It was! The comet took them right through the black hole! The ride inside it was scarier than riding a nasty, bucking bull in a rodeo. For one, it lasted much longer than eight seconds, seemingly, going on endlessly, until, it came out on the other side, where they saw this luxurious planet filled with lots of flowered bushes and evergreen trees. It had cattle, too, and they noticed a few horses scattered around. Tex let go first, then, Sam followed suit. They landed hard in a cedar tree, but didn't feel much because of the *Glazed Cowboy Lager.*

"Ouch," complained Tex. "Hey, Sam, what the hell we got here?"

"Oomph," Sam rubbed his back. "Don't know, Tex, but, I think I like it."

They jumped out of the tree, and noticed some cowboys they could see right through, just like Wyatt Earp. Tex and Sam looked at one another as they walked closer to the place. It was a scene straight from YesterStone. Sam knocked his knees together like he was about to pee, he was so excited. There was a huge corral and a beautiful Palomino stallion exercising in it. Someone was in the center with a whip, more for ordering the direction and the gait the person wanted the horse to go, than for the sting of the whip. Soon, they were joined by the ghosts of John Wayne, Roy Rogers, Tex Ritter, Audie Murphy, Gene Autry, Randolph Scot, Gary Cooper, and The Lone Ranger.

"This isn't all of us, but it's all of us who are dead," Wayne responded to their wide eyes.

"Gosh that's a gorgeous stallion," Tex said. "Mind if I go up and watch him?"

"No, go ahead. We like to keep our horses to a regimen," said Rogers. "Dead or alive. That's Trigger we're working out." A dog by his side barked," Yes, Bullet, we haven't forgotten you."

"Do you know what trail Arp was ridin' last night when he came by the OK Boreali--I mean, Saturn?" Sam asked him.

"Wyatt Earp, you mean?" he asked. Then, he pulled his guitar out from a saddle bag he had hanging over the corral fence. Sam interrupted him. "Yes, that's him," Sam said.

Tex walked back about this time.

Roger's just strummed a key and started to sing: "Some trails are happy ones, others are blue/ It's the way you ride the trail that counts..."

"My gosh," said Tex." One of Roger's old tunes."

"We aren't gonna get nothin' outta him. Them ole tunes are tellin' us nothin' we need to stick to our *goal,*" said Sam.

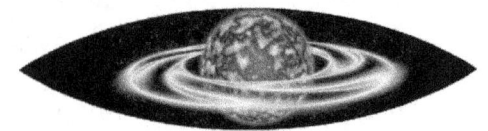

They couldn't believe how much it looked like YesterStone. There was even a bunkhouse filled with guitars, and tables strewn with cards; outside a good old-fashion wrestling, area, and even stumps for sitting at night, where you could talk about matters that concerned you during the day (no point in having whiskey like on Yester Stone; it would just go right through the ghosts. Tex and Sam pined for some, though). That's where, on the first night, Sam brought up 55 Cancri e.

"Ah just read up on a planet outside our solar system that's half solid and half liquid fire. You guys know anythin' 'bout that?" Sam asked.

They each eyed one another like they were complicit in some sort of secret. Sam

and Tex looked around at all of them.

"Say, where is Wyatt Arp? He shoulda been here with ya good guys by now?" Sam asked them.

"He's on a mission," spoke up John Wayne. "He'll be here in short order."

"Is he drivin' some crazy cattle with yellow eyes to 55 Cancri e?" Sam asked.

Gene Autry swung his guitar around to challenge Sam's guess. "He's where the longhorn cattle feed/

on the lowly gypsum weed . . ." Autry tried to sing a distraction.

Tex and Sam looked at each other befuddled.

"Well, ah'll be damn," said John Wayne. "How'd ya know?"

"Just a wile gess," answered Sam

It seems it took an eternity for Wyatt Earp to arrive, and they told him so.

"Boys," he said, "don't go talking eternity until ya know somth' about it."

Earp put them in their places: Tex looked down; Sam looked away.

"It's just that we're itching to go to 55 Cancire," Sam blurted out.

Earp looked at them like he'd been shot by a big-ball pistol; one that causes a slow, painful death.

"What?" he asked in disbelief. "Nobody WANTS to go there," he exclaimed. "For one thing the temperature will roast you alive just going near the place."

"How do *you* do it?" asked Tex.

"I'm dead that's how." Earp answered, and walked away.

"There's gotta be a way we can get over there without roasting," Sam said.

"What's the temperature range of our space spacesuits?" asked Tex.

"If ah 'member right it'll take up to 250 degrees celsius and no more." Sam figured.'

"Well, that's not nearly enough." sighed Tex.

"Nah, it ain't. We gotta figure somethun' else out. And ah don't think we're gonna get help out of any of these cowboys." Sam said, dejectedly.

"I think your right, Sam," Tex hung his head. "And, I tell ya, I'm really worried about the horses, too. They'd have to be horses from here--already dead. I'm not for roasting horses."

"Of course, they'd be from here. We have no other choice 'bout that," Sam said.

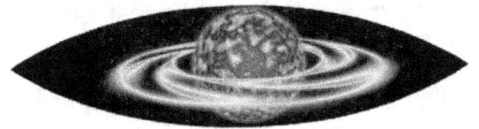

After thinking about it long and hard, they realized they have do this alone, unless they could get some help from SpaceX. So, as much as they hated to, they had to call SpaceX and tell them their predicament. First, SpaceX needed to know the planet they were on. When the ghosts told them it was called Cowboy Heaven, well, SpaceX, "said there was no such planet." When Sam and Tex told them how they got there, they said, "No one has ever been through a black hole before.

Besides, which black hole was it?" That's when they knew they'd have to find a way to do this all alone, but how? They looked at one another like they already knew how. First, they had to have a cowboy meeting to make sure, Hell, they couldn't even tell someone how to come and get them. They were going to have to die here, and they knew it. They thought about who they would miss.

Tex thought about Rocky, and his ex-wife, Millie. They'd been divorced now for three years. No kids. No worries. Well, he hadn't been as sweet on her as he had been on his horse, anyway, so that wouldn't be a great loss. He lost both his parents to cancer some years back, so at least they wouldn't miss him, and he had a good-for nothin' brother he wouldn't mind missing, either. Tex received a grant to become an aerospace engineer. This was his second job in space, and he wasn't thrilled with it, anyway.

Sam had lived a loner's life, so he had nothing to miss other than bills, women, drinking and playing poker with friends. No one would miss him, since he was an orphan who worked on his own to become a crop-dusting pilot. He got this job during the COVID epidemic when the commercial industry was shorthanded. He applied for it at SpaceX and got really lucky that he knew an airline mechanic. And, hell, he hated the Borealis.

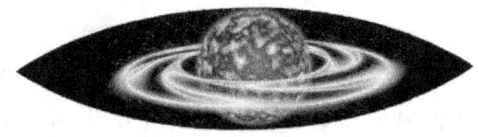

So, they rounded up the ghosts. "You guys miss anything 'bout bein' alive, like girls, raisin' hell, carryin' heat--and usin' it, good ole brawls, gunfights, you know, that sort of thing?" asked Sam.

They all looked at one another like "what's this all about"?

"Well," said Wayne, "when we died all those desires disappeared. So, I guess the answer is no."

"Not even girls?" Sam asked. "Are you kidding me? Not even women? Remind me, Tex, why I'm here," said a very disgruntled, Sam, kicking the dirt.

"We're here because we wanted to do something daring in space," answered Tex.

"I just can't believe I'm the one intentionally giving up women," Sam said.

"Then just pretend you're a man of God sworn to celibacy," Tex suggested. "You know we can't get back, so it's a little late to pine for something you'll never get again anyway."

Sam was looking "gravely" ill right about then. It was time, Sam and Tex conferred.

They were stuck, and they knew it. That damn comet came racing by when Tex was half-drunk, then, they made that stupid bet, and of all the damn times to lasso something it was then. Now they've been through a black hole they can't even name and are on a planet that doesn't exist. They saw no way out. But, how would they die and how would they know which place they would go: to Heaven, to hell hell or to Cowboy Hell? If they remained on the Enceladus alive, they would have continued to age, but they knew what life would be like. So many questions, with no answers. May as well flip a coin.

"We can't even be thrown by a ghost horse onto our heads," Sam said.

So, it was back to the drawing board to figure out how to die on this ghost planet.

"We can't commit suicide because we'd go straight to hell," said Tex.

"That's right, so, unless ya got somthin' wrong with your mind," Sam answered, "that's just what we want," Sam answered.

"Yeah, but, if we do that, how do we know it'll be Cowboy Hell and not hell hell?" asked Tex.

"Ah reckon it's cuz we *are* cowboys, duh," said Sam.

"We don't know for sure, Sam; I guess it's time for another meetin'," replied Tex.

So, they rounded them all up again. All the ghosts stood around looking a bit miffed.

"Could we hurry this time? I've got calves to brand," stated The Lone Ranger?"

"Well, hell." Sam cursed. "We need to know if we are cowboys or not; any of ya boys know of anyone who might be per – what's the word, Tex?"

"Perceived."

"That's it, 'perceived' as a cowboy, but ain't really one?" asked Sam.

"Oh sure," said Wayne. "There's Clint Eastwood, for one."

"Eastwood?!" exclaimed Tex. "I thought you were just waitin' for him to die."

"Nope. He just plays at being a cowboy. He's not a real cowboy," offered Wayne.

"But you play at being a cowboy, too," countered Tex.

"Ever see me playing anything else?"

"No, I guess not," Tex admitted.

"The same goes for Roy Rogers, Tex Ritter, Gene Autry, and The Lone Ranger," said Wayne.

"What bout Gary Cooper?" asked Sam.

"Oh, he's a cowboy at heart," Wayne smiled.

You could see the relief flow over Tex and Sam, quickly followed by confusion,

Maybe Arp confused me with Tex. Tex lives more of the cowboy life than I do, thought Sam; he looked worried.

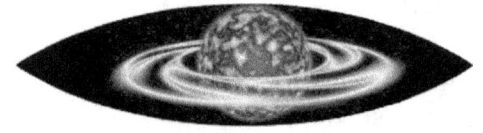

So, they decided to ask Gary Cooper. They turned to face him, "How does God know if you're a cowboy at heart?"

"Are you?" he asked.

They looked at one another. "Are we?" Tex asked Sam.

"It's a lil late to ask now, if we decided to off ourselves," he answered.

"Man. What we gonna do now?" asked Tex.

Sam said, "Somethin'll hit us; ah just know it will,""

It was at that moment that a medium-sized meteor smashed on the planet right on top of Sam and Tex.

"I never saw it coming." John Wayne told Gary Cooper.

"Me neither," said Cooper.

"Well, that's too bad, "Wayne told Cooper, "I liked the guys."

"Maybe we'll see them up here. If they were cowboys at heart."

"Hope so." said Wayne.

Sam asked the Angel Gabriel, "Why is it taking so long?"

"Gotta get the paperwork in order," said Gabriel.

"Good Go--" Gabriel looked up sharply, one brow furled.

"I mean gosh," corrected Sam, "ya guys have paperwork up here, too?!"

"You don't know the half of it," replied Gabriel stapling sheets.

Sam sat back and waited for Gabriel to finish. "Ya can't tell me 'bout Tex Ropercheaux can ya?"

"We don't discuss other clients," Gabriel answered him.

So, Sam had to leave it up to fate, or God, or whatever.

Next, was Tex's turn with the Angel Gabriel. "Since you're a Cajun, why do they call you Tex?"

"It's shorter," he answered, which wasn't quite good enough for the Angel.

"But they could call you Frenchie," he said.

"Two syllables to one," Tex answered.

Okay, Gabriel could see he was going no place with that. "So, I see that you've killed more than your share of crawfish, alligator and fish."

"If it was more than my share it was for friends or family. I'd never waste crawfish, gator or fish," said Tex, who felt like he was being questioned for the Inquisition.

"And the same with dove, quail, deer and the wild hogs you've killed?"

"Damn right. Oh, excuse me your highness, or your grace, or your, well, whatever." Tex felt flustered

Gabriel stamped his papers, stapled them and handed them to him.

"Congratulations, Cowboy Ropercheaux." he told him, and smiled.

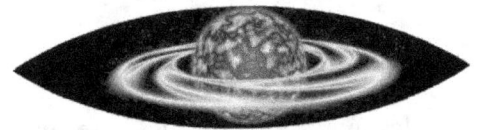

Sam had waited for Tex. When they met up, they turned to walk away, but didn't really know where to go. It felt like they had just graduated from Notre Dame.

"Since we are ghosts now, just a minute. I wanna try somthin," said Sam. He thought of Marilyn Monroe in a very compromising position. Nothing happened.

"I guess they were right when they said being a ghost would kill all your desires." He felt sad.

"I was just tryin' ta--"

But, at that very moment, the men were whisked away to Cowboy Heaven.

Tex Ritter about fell off the log he was sittin' on when they appeared.

"Guess you guys made it, although that meteor didn't leave you with much of a choice," said Wayne.

"No, Sir, it didn't," Tex agreed.

"Well, now that you've got your wings, hope they're really what you wanted." Scott said. "Not everybody really likes the cowboy life."

"Sure beats paintin' fer the Borealis," said Sam.

"You know, some of us here are painters?" Randolph Scott continued.

"Really?" asked Tex. "I'da never taken you for a painter. I'd be interested in seeing what you'd have to offer. Are any of Mae West?"

Scott smiled. "Nah, Ah paint landscapes and would love to show you a few,"

Sam interrupted them. "I'm more interested in getn' to Cowboy Hell and seein' what it's like out there,"

Earp told him becoming a ghost helped him speak better.

Sam just looked at him like he didn't know he spoke poorly in the first place. He didn't know whether to thank him or hit him, but then he remembered he couldn't hurt him so why waste a punch?

"Anyway, we have to have a 'Come ta Satan' meetin' first. Can't just someone barge into Satan's territory without knowing what they're doing and how to act," Earp warned.

That got their attention for sure.

"You mean we can't just ride down there with you and see the place?" asked Sam.

"That's a no and a no. You can't just ride down there with me, and you can't just see the place."

"Why not? I mean, how will we know where it is? And, what could be our reason for going if we aren't driving a herd of wild, devil cattle?" Tex asked.

"The gettin' there is easy. You just ride due east then follow the heat."

"An' the why?" asked Sam

"You'll have to wait for us to confer. I'll tell you tomorrow what we recommend." Earp told them.

That night in the bunkhouse Sam and Tex whispered to one another. Tex started the dialogue, throwing the covers aside. "What kinds of reasons do they have to discuss, do ya think, Sam?"

Sam rolled over, "Ahm wonderin' if we see Satan. From what he said about 'not just seeing the place' ahm thinking we do. Ah sure don't want to, do you?"

"NO! I sure DO NOT!" Tex griped emphatically.

"Ah just wished I knew what they recommended right now," Sam concluded.

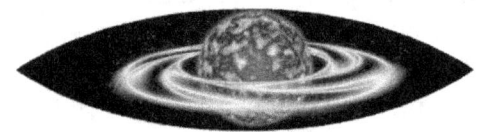

The next morning, Earp pulled them to the side and said, "Ya might have noticed that my pistols were visible—*real*, that night I rode by."

"Yes, Sir," said Tex. We did, along with a lariat. So what was the lariat for?"

Earp ignored the question for now.

"As ya get near hell, ya have to prove to Satan ya and your horses are souls; so, shoot your horse then yourself," said Earp.

"Oh, man, I don't know that I could shoot--even a ghost horse," cried Tex, "especially Trigger!"

"That's what we had to deliberate about. We figured ya were sweet on horses because ya were so attentive to Trigger, and the softer side of ya liked to paint. So we have decided to give Sam 3 bullets to your 1; Sam'll shoot your horse, his then himself."

He turned to Tex. "You'll only have to shoot yourself."

Tex lowered his head. "Thank you, Sir."

Earp continued, "That's our decision, and its final. If he doesn't hear shots by the time ya come to the end of our solar system, he'll kill ya himself, which mean she'll throw ya into the fire like he does all the bad cowboy souls. It's a brutal death

that melts the soul in less than a minute."

The men's eyes grew wide with fear.

"Now the lariat. Stay over the solid area. If anything happens, like one of ya gets thrown off your horse, ya'll have to rescue the other with the rope. Since Tex is the roper, he should carry it, especially since he has more experience both riding and lassoing. Now, as to the why, just tell one another, while you are there, you are interested in seeing Satan's trophies. Say it nice and loud. He'll be more than proud."

"An' how will we know that we are gettin' close to the end of the solar system," asked Sam, attentively.

"Ya look for the Eastern Star; it'll be the brightest star in the universe. It's also called Sirius."

"Oh, I know Sirius! It's also called Alpha Canis Major, just outside our solar system and getting closer." interrupted Tex.

"That's right. That's it." Earp concluded that part.

"Now, about how you're getting there; I see Tex is very interested in horses, I presume he can ride. How 'bout you, Sam?"

Sam put his foot on the bottom board of the fence. "A little."

"Let's give ya a mare and a week to learn to ride, then we'll see ya guys off." After a week's time, some of the ghost cowboys met Sam and Tex at the corral with their pick of hoses.

Rogers said, "We chose this experienced App mare for you that you've been practicing on, Sam. She can withstand a lightning bolt and not jolt, so we think she's just what you need. How does she feel in the saddle?"

"Like any other horse I've ridden."

"Does that include the one you put your quarter in at the grocery store?" Tex asked, kind of ashamed he made a joke at his buddy's expense. Everybody laughed out loud but Sam, who turned a bright red.

Just watching him practice, though, everybody knew those other horses he referred to were few and far between.

The only other horse in there was Trigger.

"So, where's my horse. You gonna bring him out for me to see?" Tex asked.

"We have," said Rogers.

Tex's eyes grew wide. "Trigger?! You want me to ride *Trigger*?" He was both nervous and honored. It left him speechless.

"You'll do just fine on him," Rogers assured Tex.

Earp both informed and warned them, "Ya'll ride out tonight. Now don't forget,

that extreme heat causes turbulence, which means the atmosphere will wave like a bumpy road."

Sam tried to regain his pride. "Ya'll aren't to worry 'bout us. We got this."

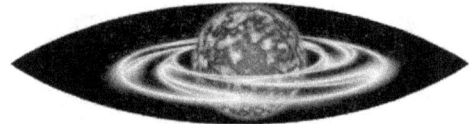

Tex and Sam kept their eyes on the sunset. The Eastern Star would be rising soon. They knew their ride would be a long one going from west to east. They had their gear, what little of it they needed, checked and rechecked.

They'd borrowed two pistols and practiced shooting with them; they also borrowed the holsters to carry them in; they both had practiced their lassoing until they were satisfied with it.

They'd saddled their horses, tightened the cinches and put on the bridles. All was at the ready. When Earp gave them the go ahead, they climbed on their mounts, Tex tipped his hat and they waved to the ghosts in the distance. They were off.

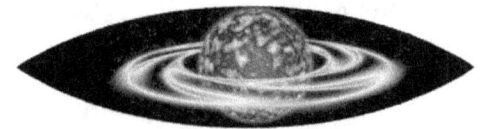

It seemed like they rode forever before they saw that Eastern Star get bigger than the Sun. Tex pointed to the Orion Constellation and pointed out the

Betelgeuse star, then the hunter's, Orion's, belt and how that led to the Sirius star. All Sam could think about was how his rear end was sure getting sore right about that time.

Then, Tex pointed to the Dog, Constellation, or Canis Major, and the Sirius star on the "dog's collar," all of which, of course, was the Eastern star. When they felt the heat, Sam decided this was a good time to do it while Tex was preoccupied with stars and constellations. He pulled his pistol before Tex saw him do it and shot

Trigger first. Tex jumped, but he was really glad Sam did it when he wasn't aware it was coming. Of course, because Trigger was a ghost, the bullet went right through his head. Sam shot through his mare then through himself. That gave Tex the courage to shoot through himself, as well. They rode on for just a mile or two, Tex continuing to talk about the Constellations, and the fact that the Cassaiopeia Constellation was a remnant of a super nova with a new star called Nova Cas 2021, which he also pointed to. Then they, finally, reached Cowboy Hell. They knew because of all the lava that hissed and boiled. It pleased them that they would never have to encounter Satan, though Earp told them he'd know they were there.

The place was hideously dismal, smoke rising from the lava, the stench of death surrounding them.

They saw a number of old tombstones, half buried, crooked, lying broken or half mired in the gooey mud. "Satan's trophies," Earp had called them, and they repeated 'nice and loud'. They were able to read some of the names, though it was mighty dark, written in blood, presumably in their own blood: Billy the Kid, Butch Cassidy, Belle Star, Jesse James, Sam Bass, Jim Miller, Bob Dalton, John Daly, Wild Bill Hickok, Bud Newcombe, and Texas Jack Hughes, for a few. For some, they couldn't read the whole name, but having heard of them, they could figure the rest of the name out. They were surprised about the woman, but they guessed women could be killers, too.

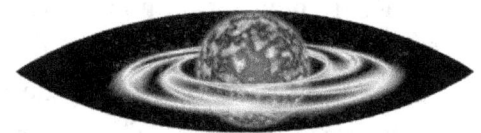

Before they left, Sam said, "Ah want to see the lava up closer, since the heat can't hurt me," so he kicked at his mare to get a little closer to at it. That's when the extreme heat caused turbulence, which surprised the mare, and she threw him. Sam could barely hang onto the solid part of hell.

"Help, Tex!" Sam shouted.

"Oh, gosh, Sam, hang on! I'm coming!"

Tex swirled his lasso over his head three times and threw it over Sam's head.

"You'll have to let go of one hand to let it drop over your waist, then exchange hands to let it drop over the other side," instructed Tex.

"Ah don't know if I can do that, Tex. Ah, like, need both hands to hold on."

"Your only other choice is to let me pull you up by the neck," responded Tex.

"That's a helluva choice," squirmed Sam.

"Which'll it be? Decide quick."

"By the neck, ah guess; just tell me right when you're gonna do it. Not second earlier or later."

"Okay, let me get this rope around the saddle horn." Tex answered him.

"Hurry!" pleaded Sam.

Just as soon as the rope was wrapped around the saddle horn Tex hollered, "NOW!"

He could hear an "umph" and continued to back Trigger. When Sam had been pulled onto "dry" land, Tex jumped off his horse and hurried over to help him loosen the rope. It took a while for Sam's face to regain its usual color, and for his voice to lose its raspiness, otherwise, their adventure had, indeed, been a success.

"Is that daring enough for you, Sam?" Tex asked, rolling his lriat back up.

"Oh, yessr it wuz," Sam's voice trembled. All they had left to do at this point was saddled up and turn their horses' heads back toward Cowboy Heaven.

"Well, Sam, while we are riding here among the stars on our way back, is there any particular star you'd like to see?" Tex asked.

"Yeah. I'd really like to see me that Taylor Swift Star," Sam answered.

"Taylor Swift, huh?" Tex looked at him.

"Well, a guy can dream, can't he?" Sam seemed irked that Tex asked.

"I don't know; can you, Sam? Dream, I mean? Have you tried lately?"

"Have you?" asked Sam

"Yep."

"Can you?" Sam looked with wide eyes.

"Nope."

"Dang."

CHASING

A GHOST

PEGGY MARCEAUX

CHASING
A GHOST

In the seedy underbelly of Chicago, Billie Mac rose one morning depressed, again. He vowed this would be the last morning he would feel this way, but he wanted to leave his sister something after he did it. He knew he couldn't bequeath her money if he took his own life, *s*o, he pulled out his treasured George Washington Saddle Pistol and wrote Heather a note.

Please forgive me, Heather. I'm sick of my head issues—all these dark mornings with hallucinations all the time. I took pills for ten years, and all for naught. I'm leaving you a pistol that is very rare; if you don't like it, you can always sell it. But, if you do, I can't promise you I won't come back to haunt you.

Love you, lil sis,
big bro, Billie

Billie then placed the barrel of his shotgun in his mouth and wedged his big toe on the trigger. Thoughts about what he was doing raced through his head. Fear, guilt, weakness… the emotions flushed over him, but the smell of the barrel wafted into his nose. In his mind, this was for the best, so he pushed those feelings out and pressed his toe down on the trigger.

Looked like and an open and shut suicide case. But, Detectives Shackles and Cuffems knew Billie Mac's background; their biggest clue was that note to his sister layin' crumpled up on the floor. That, plus his George Washington Saddle Pistol was gone. They read up on the .71 caliber pistol and learned that it was a rare, ornate, flint-lock Lafayette had been given to Washington in 1750; that placed its value in the millions. They further learned that Billie Mac spent almost every evening at the *Have Stage, Will Sing*, with the other hardened criminals in the area, who frequented the place, so the case rose pretty high on their homicide list.

"Hell," said Detective George Shackles, "any of those guys woulda loved to get his hands on that pistol, and, you know, Billie was having so many psychiatric problems he'd be an easy set-up for a suicide."

"Yep," confirmed Lieutenant Casey Cuffems, "it's more a robbery case than it is a murder case when you consider who he hung around with."

"Well, there was no powder residue from Billie Mac's hands, but there wouldn't be. Let's get the finger prints from that shotgun before we go flashing our badges," suggested Shackles, and he poured himself a cup of coffee.

"Right," agreed, Cuffems, who popped the lid of a diet, caffeine-free, soda can.

When the finger prints came back, they showed only Billie Mac's.

"Well, let's head out for the night club," said Shackles. "Stop at the convenience store so I can get me some tens."

"You figurin' on getin' some action from one of those girls at the night club?"

"I'm not interested in action. I'm on duty, remember? I'm hoping to get some info from one of those girls," Shackles responded, who poured himself another cup. "Want some?" he offered Cuffems.

"Then you'll need twenties, or maybe fifties," Cuffems stated.

"Hmmm, you're probably right." agreed Shackles. "Now, again, you want some coffee?"

"No, thanks. And, let's stop by your house to get an unmarked car," Cuffems further suggested.

"Well, I know you're right about that idea," replied Shackles.

So, they pulled into Shackles' drive to switch out cars and went to the night club incognito--no badges nor guns visible. Thy entered the place, tryin' not to be overly conspicuous, though it was difficult, for they were new to the place and, there, on the stage danced and sang a "woman", flat-chested and heavy--bearded. What was very surprising was that most of the men were filling *her* jar on stage.

"Correct me if I'm wrong here, Cuffems, but isn't this taking this same-sex thing a little too far?"

"No, it's not, Shackles, if that's what the men want. Thing is, *why* do they want it?"

Before they could get too far into the place this nice-looking young woman stepped through the curtain with what looked like a broken nose. That stopped them up short. She had a robe covering her work clothes.

"What happened to you, Sweetheart?" asked Shackles.

"Oh, I ran into a door," she replied, taking a seat at the bar.

"I'm sure you *did*," Cuffems said sarcastically. "Do you know which one of girls Billie Mac came to hear on a regular basis?" Cuffems tried to be nicer.

"Why do you say 'came', like he is dead or something?" She returned the question.

"Well, because he is dead." reported Shackles as gently as he could report something that. "It seems he took his own life last night."

She was visibly shaken. "He always came to hear me."

"Is that why you ran into the 'door' you *say* you ran into? Somebody tryin' to shut you up?" Cuffems challenged her.

She turned red and dropped her head.

"Do you have any information you can discretely share with us? We are Detective and Lieutenant Shackles and Cuffems," Shackles introduced themselves and pointed to each of them.

"No, I don't know anything," she said without looking up.

"What's your name, Sweetheart? I've told you ours?" Shackles asked her.

"Gi Gi," she said and looked up again.

"When you're ready to press charges against that 'door,' you just let us know." Cuffems threw some money on the counter to pay for her drink.

Then, they turned their attention back to the bearded singer/dancer.

"Let's mosey over and see if we can find out what's going on," suggested Shackles.

As this "woman" danced around and sang, men shoved $50's and $100's with their names written on the bills, into "her" jar and vocally alerted "her," to their bid.

Cuffems and Shackles had long been suspicious something would be going on over here, and this just confirmed it. Men were starting to thin out by the time it neared the hundred-thousand-dollar mark. Shackles tried to intervene.

"Hey, what's so special about the woman with the beard that makes her worth that kind of money?" Shackles asked a patron.

"Well, the fact that "she" owns a George Washington Saddle Pistol that's listed for more than two million dollars, that's what. It's sure isn't the beard," he laughed.

"A saddle pistol?" Shackles knitted his brows, tilted his head and played totally ignorant of the prize.

"Yeah. It's a special one," answered the patron.

"Well, no wonder I've never heard of it," Shackles shrugged his shoulders and took another sip of his drink.

Playing his part, Cuffems staggered over right about then. "Any trash on the cash, Flash?"

"Don't call me that in here, Cuffems. Patrons could hear you, besides it's too unprofessional."

"It's hard to feel professional at a night club." Cuffems admitted.

"Well, the dancer has just 'exited stage left,' so we need to get in the car and follow him/her—er—it. *And right when I need some more coffee,* he thought.

They left the club as unobtrusively as possible, which called for Cuffems to

stagger a bit.

"You're having way too much fun with this assignment," observed Shackles. Cuffems plopped in the passenger's seat, smiled and said, "Give it some gas, Flash."

They pulled in behind the black Suburban, with just enough distance between them not to excite suspicion. They also took notice of the rusty gate around the place. When the car stopped, and the passenger got out to open the gate and let the car onto the drive, the rusty hinges squeaked noticeably, even though the unmarked car's windows were up. The two officers waited a little ways down the road to make sure the car stayed, and didn't double back, then, after some more time, drove by again to get the house number. When they returned to headquarters the officers pulled out the picture line--up and looked through the mug shots.

"Here he is!" exclaimed Cuffems. "A criminal with a lengthy rap sheet. His name is Rusty Gates."

"Yep, there he is, beard and all. Wonder how much he got for that stolen pistol?" Shackles stated. "Whatever it was, it was dirty money."

"I think it's time we find out." Cuffems answered him.

They planned to leave the police station around six in the morning to beat him leaving home for any reason, but a call came in first. Seems there'd been a shooting at that address earlier that morning, and one person was reported dead. They looked at one another.

"Somebody got greedy and got there before we did. Happens all the time with the likes of him," remarked Cuffems.

"Dunno. Let's go see," said Shackles putting the coffee carafe back down on the warmer.

Cuffems followed Shackles out the door and into the squad car. Within fifteen minutes they saw the ambulance and junior officers putting out yellow crime-scene tape,

"What's the scoop, sleuth?" Cuffems asked a junior officer. Shackles just choked down a sip and stared at Cuffems who shrugged and smiled. When they walked into the bedroom, it was noticeably cold.

"Brrrr, So, do they sleep with an air conditioner set on thirty-two degrees or *what*?" shivered Cuffems.

"Yeah, it's eerily cold in here," responded Shackles. "Well, it seems we have a man, shot point blank in his sleep; his wife, sleeping right next to him, and no one in the house heard anything else but the shot. Plus, the pistol is still here on the bed."

Cuffems' mouth suddenly dropped open. "You're kiddin' me? The pistol is still here!" Cuffems exclaimed.

"They said they saw no one enter, nor exit. All that was found was a pretty, but strange-looking old pistol lying on the bed," one of the junior officers reported.

"Yep. We're gonna dust it for prints," another announced.

All they saw besides the pistol was a lot of blood, presumably all from Rusty Gates. No evidence of footprints, either inside or outside the premises. No evidence of forced entry; Rusty kept his home both locked and padlocked, for obvious reasons. In addition, Rusty had cameras both inside and outside his house. Both the detective and lieutenant were foaming at the mouth to see those.

"Interesting case," said Shackles. "Don't know that I've had one like it before."

"I sure haven't," said Cuffems. "Not one shred of evidence at the scene. Really counting on that film."

"Let's take another ride to the night club. I want to check out something," said Shackles. "Plus, I can get another cup of coffee on the way."

"Beats me how you sleep at night with all that caffeine." Cuffems turned to look out his door window.

When they arrived, there was a bouncer at the door this time. He was all muscled up like someone who visited the gym regularly. Shackles showed his badge. "What's your name, fella?"

"What's it to you?" and the bouncer stood with his arms crossed, looking formidable.

"It's to clear you of Rusty Gate' murder."

"Figured you guys would be back here. Look, I had nothing to do with that."

Cuffems flashed his badge. "Name?"

"The bouncer looked him in the eyes, "Buster," he said.

"Buster what?" asked Cuffems.

"Buster Nose." Cuffems almost jumped him, but Shackles held him back. "I'm not through with you," Cuffems said to the bouncer."

When they walked inside, Shackles began to look for the informant who had told him about the bearded man and the George Washington Saddle Pistol. He was told by the bar tender that Louis Tongue had encountered "an unfortunate demise," and that he wouldn't be coming in again.

"What about Gi Gi?" asked Cuffems.

"She should be healed very soon," the employee offered, encouragingly.

"She'd better be, or I'm—"

Shackles hushed him and pulled him away.

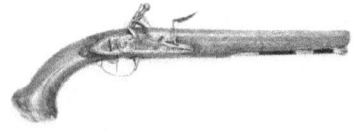

Shackles and Cuffems left the place and pondered the situation on the drive back to look at the film inside and outside of Gates' house.

"The no footprints stumps me," said Shackles, taking a sip of cold coffee from his paper cup.

"Leaving the gun there puts me in a quandary," and Cuffems scratched his head.

When they arrived at the office, they were both eager to get to that film.

"Let's go straight to the film in the bedroom. No since in prolonging what we don't have to know," announced Shackles, pouring himself some more hot coffee.

"I'm with you on that. Oh, no thank you," he told Shackles who offered him some.

Instead, he popped himself another can of decaffeinated soda. They were both speechless when they saw the film, for they saw the gun being removed from its case, moving through the air to the bed and shooting Mr. Gates, *all on its own*.

Shackles and Cuffems both looked at one another in disbelief, their mouths open. They sat there for a few minutes. Finally, Cuffems broke the silence. "Did I truly see what I just saw?"

"If you saw a ghost shoot Mr. Gates, you did," replied Shackles.

"Then, no need to expect anything from finger print analysis. All we'll find is Mr. Gates, and the rightful owner, Billie Mac," Cuffems stated.

Shackles let out a heavy sigh. "Gates could have let someone look it over. At least we'd have someone to warn," he said.

"And, say what? There's a ghost that'll probably come calling? I don't think so. Besides. I don't know if I can believe my eyes, yet," Cuffems leaned back in his chair. "If you don't mind, I'll take that coffee now. Black."

They needed an informant in the worse way, but Shackles' man was dead, or permanently unavailable. Getting past the bouncer was easier this next time, though he still got Cuffems' hackles up. Perhaps Gi Gi could help them. They were at her performance that night. Her poor nose still bandaged, but the owner of the club wasn't worried. He thought that's the last thing men would be looking at. And, he was probably right. They stuffed tens in her jar as she sang and danced as long as she sang and danced, then asked a word with her behind the curtain.

"Gi Gi," asked Cuffems, "Did you see anyone inspect the pistol Gates was trying to sell that night?"

"I did see Jack look it over before Gates left. He wanted the pistol, but, if I know Jack; it was way out of his price range," she answered.

"Do you know his last name?" asked Shackles.

"Asser. But, please don't tell anyone. They don't give us insurance here," she begged.

"You're not to worry. And, when you want to press charges against Buster Nose, I'm here for you. All you have to do is say," Cuffems assured her.

The next day, when they went back to the police station, they picked out his mug shot easily. "Looks like a Jack Ass, doesn't he?" Cuffems observed.

"Well, I'll withhold judgment until I hear him bray," answered Shackles, and they both got a hardy laugh at Jack's expense.

By the time they arrived at Jack's farm, he was already gone. "To that damn night club," his wife had said.

All they truly remembered about that visit was hearing the donkey bray before they got back into the squad car. They had to laugh out loud. Once past the bouncer again, they found Jack sitting in the night club. They flashed a badge and pulled him aside.

"Did you hear about Rusty Gates," Shackles asked him .

"Yeah, but I hope you guys don't think I had anything to do with that. All I did was inspect the gun."

"No, we know you didn't. We're just here to warn you that the perpetrator might be targeting you next," said Cuffems.

"Me?"

"Yes, but that's all we can say. So, watch your back," they told him and walked toward the door. Cuffems stuffed a twenty in Gi Gi's jar on his way out, and she smiled at him.

"Now what?" asked Cuffems. "Where do we go with this investigation?"

Neither spoke all the way to the station. The next morning, at about 3:00, they were both awakened with a phone call. Jack Asser had been shot dead by that George Washington Saddle Pistol. And, they both woke with the same reply: "But, how?"

"We retained that firearm as evidence at the station," Shackles told his wife.

Before they drove to Asser's farm, each arrived at the station around 4:15 to check the evidence room. Sure enough, the pistol was missing.

"We've got ourselves a rat in the department," stated Cuffems.

All Shackles could do was purse his lips and wonder who.

They agreed that Cuffems would drive to Asser's while Shackles would start to investigate his own department. It was no easy task. Shackles looked through all the recent applicants for the department and found one member he wasn't familiar with--a fellow by the name of Ryker Riggedit. He made some discrete calls and didn't like what he heard. When Cuffems returned he heard virtually the same thing that they learned with Gates' murder. All but one thing—the pistol was gone this time.

Shackles told Cuffems, "Well, I can tell you who will be next, this time."

"Brrrr," said Cuffems. "You can investigate at the residence for the next murder, if there *is* a next one. Either that or I'm gonna need a warmer coat."

"I need a cup of coffee'" said Shackles.

"Get me one, too, please. Scalding hot and black."

When the call came in this time, it was closer to midnight. It told them that Ryker Riggedit was murdered in his bed, just like the others, and, again, the weapon was missing.

Cuffems put his head down. "I just don't know how to chase a ghost, Shackles."

"I don't either, but it's our job to try," concurred Shackles

Heather, Billie Mac's sister, who was allowed to read her brother's suicide note, had been following the case closely. After six weeks, when it seemed it had stalled, she hired a Private Eye named Fleece de

Soul, who enlisted a Wilma Witch to get the pistol for her by way of a Séance. It did the trick. Heather was more than pleased to have her pistol back, sold it to a man named Scott Plot Twist, paid Fleece de Soul and Wilma Witch what they were asking, and had some left to pay off her and her husband's debts--all with dirty money, of course. After her debts were paid, she started getting back into owing as soon as she could by over-charging on her credit cards; Billie Mac started to haunt her for the rest of her life.

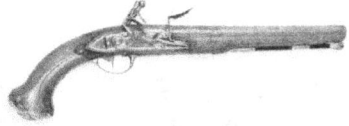

Meanwhile, after a rainy night, Scott Plot Twist had visited the office of Shackles and Cuffems. He quietly entered, shot Shackles dead at point blank range with his Smith and Wesson .40 and shot at Cuffems, who returned fire. Cuffems hit him in the left arm but was eventually killed, as well. The officers investigating this murder had lots of evidence to go on: spent cartridges, from Plot Twist's gun, his prints on the cartridges, blood, and foot prints to name a few; however, there was no time to find the perp, for the next morning, when he was discovered dead in his bed, the investigating officers could find nothing but a very cold room. No foot-prints, no gun, no anything that had belonged to the perp, except a .71 caliber flint lock ball in his spine. The gun ended up back at his sister's house in time. A smart girl, she kept her mouth shut about it this time, locking it securely in her safe.

They had eventually closed the case and had let it go, er,—*cold.*

But.

Then.

Sonny Honey "barger," who took Shane de Britt's place as the leader of his gang of Hell's Angels after he was killed, got a whiff of what was going around in the underworld of Chicago. They kick-started their Harleys and made the long drive from Ruidoso, New Mexico, where they'd held their last rally, to Chicago, Illinois, stopping occasionally for some Utopia beer and jerky meat. When they arrived in Chicago, they had to plan out this robbery carefully. None thought they would ever see a gun like this George Washington Saddle Pistol, much less inspect it with their own hands, so they were making meticulous plans to steal it. Sonny decided that Axel and Damon would break into Heather's house that night and find their way to the bedroom, where she probably kept the safe. There hadn't been a safe made that Damon couldn't crack. If it was possible, there would be any casualties, but that was only *if* possible.

"Let's just hope little sister and her hubby minds their Zzzz's," Sonny said and chuckled.

All went as planned, and Heather woke to a safe both broken into and wide open. She called the robbery in to the police department, but was none too confident. When the Outlaws heard what the Hells Angels did, and right under their noses on their own home turf, they were livid and "loaded for bear". They revved up their bikes in their home town of Chicago, intending to cut the Angels off at the pass as they retuned back to Ruidoso, but the Angels threw them a curve by planning to drive down to California. They first drove by an all-night liquor store and robbed them of a few cases of Guinness.

The chase was on!

When they realized that the Angels got off trail, Hog, Snug 260, the leader of the Outlaws, signaled for a halt and regrouped. They did so at a liquor store south of Chicago. There were iron bars up all around the place, but they weren't worried about that.

"Okay, gang, looks like they're headed more south to southwest, so California, here we come. I don't care what state a Hell's Angel is killed in; he's just as dead. Now, Calum and Cash, I want you to hide your tattoos as best you can, amble into the store, and pick up a couple sf cases each of Dogfish Head beer. If the cashier makes any noise, flash them your Ruger. Takin' IH 57 for now. Any questions.?"

"Yeah," asked Jag. "When do we get the beer?"

"Soon as we're down the road a bit, and they can break the cases open." replied Hog.

So, they revved their bikes and were off chasing the Angels down the road to hell. They were careful to hide their weapons and ammo, but, the Outlaw and Hell's Angels tats were tell-tale signs enough to let you know there was an imminent rumble in the making.

After driving some distance, the Outlaws saw two freshly dug graves on the side the road. They stopped. "You just don't see this," spoke up Hog. "Nobody buries *people* on the side of the road. I think I recognize those names, too. Any of you hear of an Axel and a Damon?"

"Sure have. Those are Angels' men," stated Dexter. "Wonder what happened?"

And, a little ways forward they saw a grave dug with Sonny's name on it. "Well, hell," said Hog, "they are running lose with no leader. That'll be easy pickin's."

They kick started their bikes again, and were on the road chasing after a ghost, but didn't know it. They made their way to 97 then took IH 5 down into the Sacramento area.

That's where they saw a large group of hogs parked at a pub, their riders inside eating supper. Whoever of the Angels saw the Outlaws walk inside the place first punched the guy next to him. The Outlaws were curious about the graves they saw, so Hog decided to approach them, without a weapon, of course.

"What's up with Sonny, Axel and Damon?" Hog asked them.

One fella took a bite of his sandwich, and with s mouthful said, "They was shot dead by that pistol they stole from the girl."

"Which one of you did it?" asked Hog.

"Hell," he said, "ain't none of us know how to load that flint lock, and we sure don't have the powder, either."

"Can you prove they were killed by a flint lock?" asked Hog.

"Sure," said the man," swallowing his beer, "if you want to dig up the graves and search for the iron ball. We're not going to do it, because we know a ghost killed them".

"A ghost hmm?" Hog asked, with a half grin. "Then, you'll be glad we rid you of 'the curse' by letting me take the gun off you." Hog concluded.

"Nope. It stays with the Angels, no matter what," said the man with the mouthful of food.

"Well, I suggest we meet up bout high noon at Golden Canyon in Death Valley tomorrow to see who has the rights to that gun," challenged Hog.

"Okay, if you're so willing to die for it," the man with the mouthful of food said, while slurping his beer.

"I know it's worth millions, which makes it worth killin' the likes of you," Hog replied.

The rest of the men at the table stared at Hog, their brows furled and grimaces on their faces. Then, they all stood with such menacing postures the proprietor got worried.

"Oh, and be sure you have the pistol with you," said Hog. "I'd sure hate to think you'd make a game of hide and go seek out of this, when perhaps all of you would be slaughtered."

Casron moved forward to accost him, but a hand pulled him back. "Save it for Death Valley," the man who reached out to stop him said.

Guess we'll see about that ghost killer now, Hog thought to himself, chuckling, and sauntered back to the Outlaws, who by this time were eating supper, too, but on the other side of the pub. Hog relayed that the deaths of those buried on the side of the road were by pistol shot, but never blamed the gun he wanted, and he sure never even suggested the word "ghost." He told the boys of the "meet up" at Golden Canyon in Death Valley tomorrow around noon, and for them to get their weapons locked and loaded after breakfast.

"Wish we woulda known," said Dexter, "Ida had me a damn steak.'

"That's a good idea," and Hog Honey" barger" ordered the biggest steak on the menu.

"Rare, please," he told the waitress.

When the morning arrived, the Outlaws rose early and found a restaurant highly frequented for breakfast. They all had black coffee and ordered eggs, bacon, sausage patties and hash browns. None knew if this would be their last meal or not. Afterward they went back to their tents to triple check their guns, magazines, ammo, and just general over-all equipment. All seemed oiled and ready to go. They didn't bother hiding their guns this time; the law didn't want to tangle with them when they were riding to a rumble.

The Angels did something similar, but had to go to another eatery, since the Outlaws grabbed their first choice. They had fried eggs and bacon, some with pancakes all buttery and with syrup loaded on them. They left the restaurant laughing and in jovial moods, not worried at all about this rumble that would take place later that day.

The Outlaws took a lesser-known road to Death Valley in order to avoid the Angels. The Angels had put Dexter in charge of the GW Saddle Pistol, and had taken the direct route to Golden Canyon, but both gangs planned to arrive there within minutes of one another. After arriving first, the Angels ditched their bikes behind a Canyon wall, put on their hearing protection muffs, and hid out at the rear of one of the beautiful mountainous protrusions in the gulch.

The Outlaws rode in noisily next, used their binoculars to find the Angels, and perched behind a rock wall opposite them. When the first unlucky soul showed his face, a volley went off, and a Hog was appalled that his man lay at his feet with his face blown off. The Outlaws returned fire, making sure they were shooting at people and not rock formations.

The Angels did the same, dropping another Outlaw, this time near a rock cropping.

"Two to nothing," said Jag.

Hog used his binoculars again, and found where a man was peeping over the edge of a ledge. He exchanged his binoculars for his weapon and pulled the trigger. The Angel had no time to scream. Hog's men looked for another opportunity to even the score. They saw one when an Angel tried to move to another outcropping for a better advantage. One of the Outlaws, who'd been looking through their scopes for chances, spotted him. He fired and dropped him.

"Guess we're even now," said the Outlaw.

The Angels tried to be more vigilant, but to no avail, for a volley from the Outlaws surprised them when someone unsuspectingly moved positions. They sprayed off a volley through the group that killed at least six. No one was wounded; no one gets wounded when a master shoots an assault rifle.

"That a way to go, Tiger," said Hog.

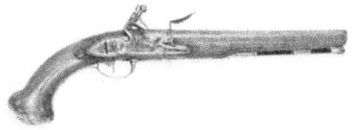

This went on all day, matching gunfire for gunfire. It was, indeed, located in Death

Valley, for all that it amounted to that day was death. The sole survivor was Hog himself, the man so hungry for that George Washington Saddle Pistol. He walked up to the outcropping from where the Angels had fired. When he saw the 1750 flint-lock he was bewitched. It was the most beautiful pistol he'd ever seen. He reached down and picked it up. "Oh. my God," he said, "a pistol like this is definitely worth a rumble." He put it in his belt, walked to his lone bike, kick-started it and rode back toward Chicago.

That next morning the police were called to a motel room on the route to Chicago. Seems a man was murdered in a freezing room as he slept. No footsteps, no forced entry, no prints anywhere in the

room, and no weapon left behind. The pistol just miraculously appeared a few days later back in his sister's safe, but she wouldn't dare handle it, much less sell, it this time.

ABOUT THE AUTHOR

Peggy Marceaux

Peggy Marceaux is a retired English teacher who lives in Canyon Lake, Texas. She earned her Bachelor's Degree from Lamar University and her Masters of Arts from the University of Houston, where she specialized in British Literature.

Ms. Marceaux taught for 32 years; 11 in the Alvin Independent School District and 15 in the Comal Independent School District in TX, Chairing the High School English Departments in both.

Having raised chickens for twenty years, she loved the diversity among the breeds. This inspired "BeakSpeak", a story designed to help young people accept their differences and build confidence, through speech validation. Ever the English teacher, Ms. Marceaux believes the earlier you teach children language precision, the better it will help them succeed in their future relationships and careers.

Along with BeakSpeak, Ms. Marceaux is also involved with CLAW the Canyon Lake Area Writers at the Tye Preston Memorial Library in Canyon Lake, Texas where they meet for two hours the first and third Tuesday of each month. They enjoy letting their creative juices flow with writing prompts, have visiting speakers import helpful knowledge, and submit their 5,000-to-8,000-word short stories to Raconteur in the hopes of gaining publicity.

About BeakSpeak – the Characters

The BeakSpeak characters are inspired from Peggy's own chickens! Some 30+ years ago Peggy began raising chickens on her farm and discovered that chickens have personalities. Along with their very personable characteristics they must learn quickly that there is a pecking order. Like human society, some chickens behave aggressively, others passively, and weak birds cannot survive a bully without a human intervening.

Her chicken coop, then became the English classroom, where Ms. Marceaux taught language skills for 32 years in high school. "My greatest reward was watching my students grow to respect one another, find their confidence, learn how to rationally think about the world around them, and then shape their views to fit in that world. I was able to help them do all this by teaching them that, when you think, speak and write precisely and concisely, using the clearest and most effective words, with the most energetic verbs to defend your views, the better you communicate your meaning."

The first BeakSpeak book is a colorful rendition of a classroom of chickens who are learning about thinking and language skills. Add to those techniques, Marceaux stimulates thought with her exploratory questions, and suggested answers. BeakSpeak, A Fable and Language Workbook is a perfect companion piece with this book as everyone can benefit from learning how to better communicate with others!

About the Author

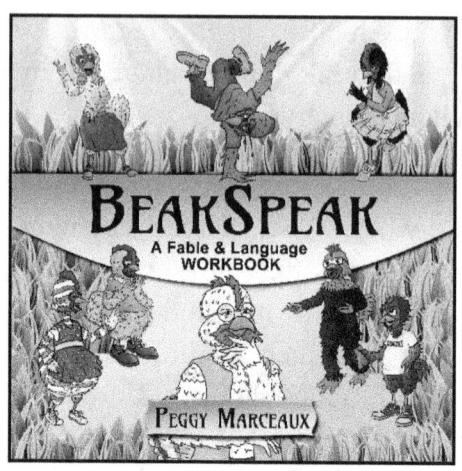

These books are available anywhere books are sold online. Learn more on
www.PeggyMarceaux.com

Erin Go Bragh Publishing publishes various genres of books for numerous authors. Their portfolio consists of a 1200-page Vietnamese to English Dictionary, Historical fiction, an award-winning children's educational series, and an array of fun children's picture books, multiple adult novels and memoires, tween adventure stories, as well as Christian Fiction. Their objective is to promote literacy and education through reading and writing.

www.ErinGoBraghPublishing.com
Canyon Lake, Texas